William Everson

DUST SHALL BE THE SERPENT'S FOOD

•

Book I: The Engendering Flood
Cantos I-IV

By William Everson

VERSE

These Are the Ravens (1935)
San Joaquin (1939)
The Masculine Dead (1942)
The Waldport Poems (1944)
War Elegies (1944)
The Residual Years (1944)
Poems MCMXLII (1945)
The Residual Years (1948)
A Privacy of Speech (1949)
Triptych for the Living (1951)
An Age Insurgent (1959)
The Crooked Lines of God (1959)
The Year's Declension (1961)
The Hazards of Holiness (1962)
The Poet Is Dead (1964)
The Blowing of the Seed (1966)
Single Source (1966)
The Rose of Solitude (1967)
In the Fictive Wish (1967)
A Canticle to the Waterbirds (1968)

The Springing of the Blade (1968)
The Residual Years (1968)
The City Does Not Die (1969)
The Last Crusade (1969)
Who Is She that Looketh Forth as the Morning (1972)
Tendril in the Mesh (1973)
Black Hills (1973)
Man-Fate (1974)
River-Root/A Syzygy (1976)
The Mate-Flight of Eagles (1977)
Rattlesnake August (1978)
The Veritable Years (1978)
The Masks of Drought (1980)
Eastward the Armies (1980)
Renegade Christmas (1981)
The High Embrace (1985)
In Media Res (1985)
Mexican Standoff (1989)
The Engendering Flood (1990)

PROSE

Robinson Jeffers: Fragments of an Older Fury (1968)
Archetype West: The Pacific Coast as a Literary Region (1976)
Earth Poetry (1980)
Birth of a Poet (1982)
Writing the Waterbirds (1983)
The Excesses of God (1988)

WILLIAM EVERSON

THE ENGENDERING FLOOD

BOOK ONE OF DUST SHALL BE THE SERPENT'S FOOD (CANTOS I–IV)

BLACK SPARROW PRESS
SANTA ROSA 1990

THE ENGENDERING FLOOD. Copyright © 1985 and 1990 by William Everson.

All rights reserved. Printed in the United States of America. No part of this book may be used or reproduced in any manner whatsoever without written permission from the publisher except in the case of brief quotations embodied in critical articles and reviews. For information address Black Sparrow Press, 24 Tenth Street, Santa Rosa, CA 95401.

ACKNOWLEDGMENTS

Of these four cantos, two have appeared previously. The first, "In Medias Res," was issued in a limited edition by Adrian Wilson from his press in Tuscany Alley in San Francisco. The second one, "Skald," appeared in *Lord John Ten*, published by Herb Yellin, commemorating the first decade of Lord John Press. The two remaining cantos appear here for the first time.

Black Sparrow Press books are printed on acid-free paper.

LIBRARY OF CONGRESS CATALOGING-IN-PUBLICATION DATA

Everson, William, 1912-
  The engendering flood : book one of Dust shall be the serpent's food (Cantos I-IV) / William Everson.
    p.   cm. — (Dust shall be the serpent's food ; bk. 1)
  Contents: In medias res — Skald — Hidden life — The hollow years.
  ISBN 0-87685-807-8 (cloth) : $20.00 — ISBN 0-87685-808-6 (signed cloth ed.) : $30.00 — ISBN 0-87685-806-X (paper) : $8.50
  I. Title. II. Series: Everson, William, 1912-   Dust shall be the serpent's food ; bk. 1
PS3509.V65D88 bk. 1
811'.52 s—dc20
[811'.52]   90-1146
                                                                              CIP

Author's Note

The Engendering Flood is the first book of an autobiographical epic poem entitled *Dust Shall Be the Serpent's Food*. It consists of four cantos, the first being called "In Medias Res," so named after the classic formula for the epic as it has come down to us from the Greek and Latin tradition. The words mean simply "in the midst of things," but more aptly have come to specify "the low point in the fortunes of the hero." For me that point was certainly the funeral of my father at the close of World War II in 1945, and so I have begun it.

The epic formula then calls for flashback to delineate how the hero got to that point. Thus Canto II, entitled "Skald," after the Scandinavian minstrels or bards of the Viking period, relates the life of my father, an immigrant Norwegian musician. Canto III, "Hidden Life," narrates the humble origin of my mother on a Minnesota farm in the last century, how she met my father and how they fell in love. Canto IV, "The Hollow Years," tells of the estrangement of the lovers, their eventual reconciliation, marriage, procreation, and arrival in Selma, California, where I grew up. Thus far, my immediate lineal background. Book Two will begin my personal odyssey.

W. E.

Contents

In Medias Res   13
Skald   25
Hidden Life   41
The Hollow Years   55

The Engendering Flood

Canto One
IN MEDIAS RES

APRIL 7, 1945, SELMA, CALIFORNIA

The bleak Masonic rite faltered to a close,
And the mourners filed out, impassively. The undertaker
Beckoned the family forward, brought round the coffin
For the final convocation, our last togetherness
Before the closing of the tomb.

                              Approaching my father's body
I felt cold constriction tighten my chest. Five years past,
Nearly five years now, in this same Masonic temple,
The family had convened, gathered round the body of our
          mother,
Stunned with the suddenness, shaken with loss.

I had stood dry-eyed, but when the lid was closed
Something snapped in my skull. In a choking
Rage, twisted by unreckonable guilt,
I pounded my fists on the coffin,
Sobbing: "Why! Why!" and slumped to my knees,
Jarring the bier.

                Lifting my face
I met the terrible gaze of my father,
Glaring across the lidded coffin—
Those Viking eyes, the awful accusation of Thor—
"You bastard! Profane the last sacred moment!
Spoil it! Go ahead! Ham it up!"

                                      I sagged to one side,
But the eyes jerked me upright, scorning:
"From the moment you were born
You took her from me, and now, at the lip of the grave,
When everything she was slips away and my life with it,
You throw your misbegotten body between!"

I crawled to my feet, dizzily erect, and spun blindly,
Sobbing shut frustration, galling guilt.
My brother and sister, seizing my arms,
Hushed me, hoarsely whispering: "Bill! Bill!"
Fearfully urgent. And with them, my wife,
Imploring, beseeching, her voice
Taut as a wire.

                I flung off their hands,
Stumbling blindly, erratic, fleeing them,
Gasping: "Leave me alone! Keep away, all of you!
Let me be!" But my father's eyes,
Back beyond the coffin, drilling from afar,

Nailed me to the wall, taunting: "Go ahead!
Rant! Ham it up! Play the heavy!"

And gathering up my will, a kind of throttling mastery,
I clenched back my sobs, swept tears from my eyes,
Choking: "Forgive me!" Then my sister, still aghast
But suddenly compassionate: "Bill, if you don't want to . . .
I mean, you don't have to go to the cemetery if . . ."
But I thrust past her: "No, I'm all right!
I want to! I have to be there!"

A long moment of awkwardness, an eternity
Of embarrassment gripped us, and we hung on it,
Inflexible, caught in a ghastly suspension—
Till suddenly the undertaker clapped his hands,
Seizing the moment to break the spell,
And the pallbearers filed in, mechanically,
Automatons of death, looking neither to right nor to left.
For something unspeakable hung in that room,
And they knew it, something not to be named,
Something indecent . . .

                We moved out, then,
Behind the wheeling coffin, saw it
Enter the darkness of the door, the shadowy threshold,
Saw it tilt down the stairs, steeply, strain forward,
Checked by the staggering pallbearers, stumbling
Awkwardly on the steps, out in the drizzling December day.

Behind the family I followed them down,
And could not but notice the mourners below
Staring up at me, open mouthed,
Painfully aware of my death-side outburst,
My shocking scene . . .

        Five long years . . .

And now, in this same Masonic temple,
I moved to my father's inscrutable coffin,
Sensing my brother and sister
Close in behind me, just in case—
But my wife not here, she far away,
Doing God knows what in San Francisco.
("God does know what," the fact flared in my mind,
"Crawling another man's bed, that's what!").

But ferociously shut down the searing thought,
Knuckles whitening in the fist's clench—
"But that's all right," I grimly concluded,
"This time no outburst, right? No hysterics.
Not this pig . . ."

        At coffin-side
I gazed down a time at the set
Composed features, unseen these many months
Since conscription claimed me;
Looked at the death-set lips that had cursed me,

The calm folded hands that had never blessed me.
Then the short torso, so faultlessly attired,
Immaculately groomed in the mortician's art,
But shockingly stilted. And felt for the first time
The mordant pang that would soon become familiar,
The wince of pain that I let my father go
Unreconciled into the grave. And a tremor
Shook through me, but nothing like what happened before,
No, nothing like that . . .

                  The coffin lid closed,
And watching it settle, my gauche outburst
Shoved from my mind, I thought how everything
Had changed, changed utterly: five hapless years
All stripped away, everything gone —
Mother gone, wife gone, father gone, vineyard gone —
Brother and sister turning back to their lives,
Their separate existences — Gone!
And I to return to my northern incarceration,
To wait out the war with the stark objectors,
Who denied the State its injunction to kill,
And paid for denial with a slave's labor.

And I looked up, taking my sister's hand,
And the hand of my brother,
And then turned aside, smiling faintly,
And said simply, smiling and turning,
"Let's go!"

        And the coffin moved.

                      Following it out
I watched it pass through the door, the shadowy threshold,
Burst into the searing sunlight beyond,
The strong light of April;
Saw it tilt down, the steep stairs taking it;
Saw the pallbearers staggering under the load,
Stumbling awkwardly on the steps,
While the massed mourners, deployed below,
Awaited its passage into the hearse.

Following it out, the straight-falling sunlight
Suddenly enveloped me, and through squinting eyes
I looked down the steps to the sea of faces,
My fellow townsmen and my boyhood friends,
Gathered in homage to the man who had led them,
Thirty years, first as bandmaster then as judge,
Thirty long years . . . I paused uncertainly there,
Balancing on the top steps, half blinded
By the sun, and let my brother descend,
My sister following.

             As the hearse
Swallowed up the stone-cold coffin
I started down, then paused, feeling unreal, floating,
For a dizziness seized my sight.
And I gazed about me, gathered focus in my mind,

And saw to my left a green cupola, the Victorian mansion
Where Jess Morgan, that affable sportsman,
Had taken his life with his own deer rifle,
And his daughter Doris, my childhood sweetheart,
Had fled this town, never to return,
Nor ever to frolic together again,
Through the long summer days on the spacious lawns,
Swinging under the mulberry trees,
Never again our eyes to meet, our secrets to share . . .

And beyond the house lay High Street,
The civic concourse, and across the way
The Carnegie Library where, night after night,
From the time I could read,
I crouched in the stacks devouring books,
Bushels of books, till the spinster librarian
Closed it at nine . . .

    And suddenly,
There on the tall steps, above the sea of faces,
Friends and townspeople, my mind
Swept out beyond the city limit
To the little cemetery, the plot where
Redolent in the earth, my mother lay buried; and beside her
The naked hole that would take down my father,
Darkly glowing, a subsumed luster,
Numinous with the haunting infusion of death . . .

And around them, dwarfing them, lay the mighty
Spread of the earth, field beyond field,
Like an inland sea, rolling,
Sweeping away to the shining mountains,
The majestic grandeur of the Pacific Slope.

And thinking of mountains I remembered my father,
The white-crowned brow—high peaked ridges athwart the
    East,
Thunderheads forming in the fierce Spring heat,
The long ranks of forest like desperate armies charging
    upslope
To the bitter timberline where the hordes fall back,
Repulsed by granite and eternal snow.

                      And suddenly I realized
I would never see it again, this world, not as I knew it.
For look, what has become of it?
Already it is changed—changed as the world within me
Had changed, as naked, as starkly unreal as my inner self;
That what swam about me, there on those steps,
Above the sea of faces and the sea of my world,
Was another dimension, another existence,
Not defined by the valley or the valley towns,
Nor the majestic realm of the Pacific Slope.

For beyond the Sierras lay a continent,
Crouched like a beast, a giant cougar

Tensing to spring, and out of that tension
The nation, its nerves coiling for the final drive,
The war sweeping toward apotheosis,
The mighty Nazi war machine
Beaten to its knees, breaking, fragmenting,
Thrown back on every front,
Europe convulsed in a tentacular paroxysm,
The powerful American sweep
Thrust deep in its vitals, boring remorselessly in;
And I, remote from it, watch and wait,
Suffering in the soul what it suffers in the flesh.

And reeling there on those tall steps
I put out my hands, as a man
Balances in a dream, giddily entranced.
And suddenly my sister started back up the stairs,
Calling "Bill! Bill!" And I realized I had turned,
Staggered, convulsively sobbing,
Tears streaming my face.

But before she could reach me
I gathered strength in a mighty effort,
And my head cleared. I straightened,
As a man straightens under a load,
And walked down the stairs, limping
But upright, straight now,
"Under my own power, by God,"

No hands sustaining me. And the faces
Of friends I no longer knew
Swam in my tear-blind eyes.

Canto Two
SKALD

DECEMBER 22, 1870, BREVIK, NORWAY

A legendary life: by the blood,
Norse, a bantam born to a race of giants,
He fell from the womb the last of twelve,
Taking his mother's life in his leap,
And bore thereafter the ineluctable sorrow,
The pall of matricide haunting his heart,
Stifling his soul, the insidious
Guilt of survival.

              Who, then, nurtured his life?
Not, for one, his dour father. That worthy fanatic
Was never around. Itinerant preacher.
Founder of his own evangelical splinter,
The Iversonians, he cast fire and brimstone
On the hummocks of Norway; yet his awesome ardor,
Not wholly quenched in apostolic zeal,
Found an opening in the mundane sector. A cobbler
         by trade
He brought the art of vulcanization
To the Norwegian people; but its raw toxicity,

Ill understood, cut him down. The ardor died
Unslaked.

         Orphaned at twelve,
My father was taken by a well-to-do aunt
To the urban ambience of the capital city:
Now Oslo by name, but then Christiania,
An awkward, Dane-derived appellation.
There he languished, mutely unhappy,
But soon came a day when a giant ship
Hove to in the harbor, riding high in the slack,
Having lately discharged its whole bill of lading
From foreign shores; but would soon
Resettle to the waterline
When the horde of emigrants boarded.

                             For these were the days
Of the great migrations, the cream of Norway's
Burgeoning populace skimmed off for the States,
A lemming-like tide of human hunger:
Wanderlust West, reliving the atavistic dream,
Leif the Lucky, the whale-haunted sea, and the lure
Of the Vinland tryst.

                 So the bustling emigrants
Surged through the streets, and he followed,
A sad-faced, tow-headed stray,
Unnoticed among them — farmers and workers,

Wives, children and mothers; infants
Slung in a shawl or hitched on the hip.
And he ran unremarked out along the wharf,
Darted up the funnelling gangplank,
Out onto the deck — almost as if
He himself were choosing the shadow-way West
(America, the wonderful word on everyone's lips),
Almost as if he too heard the call —
Fare Forward! Fare far! Almost as if
He too laid claim to a fabulous future
Uniquely his own.

        And so, small for his age,
And unobtrusive, he mixed with the throng,
Roamed the boat absorbed with its fixtures,
Instinctively shunning the fetid steerage;
Descending at last to the monstrous gut,
The beast's great groin, pulsing heart
Of the savage leviathan, the mighty turbine.
Stopped in his tracks by that awesome organ
He found a nook, sank sighing down,
And so fell asleep.

        Awake with a start
He dashed up the stairs and out onto the deck
To find it deserted, night falling fast and land gone;
Rushed to the stern where, all alone,
Looked longingly back at the widening wake

Creasing the Skagerrak, and the stormy petrel
Gleaned the sea-churn for the dark
Propeller-torn kill. Suddenly afraid
An immense forlornness swept over him.
He turned back to a bulkhead, sank down,
Great sobs shook through him, unstemmable.
Then a strong hand fell on his shoulder;
He looked fearfully up through brimming tears
To the genial face of the mate.

*

                    And a strange
Voyage they had of it. The great ship surged forward,
Shearing the deceptively flaccid sea. At summer solstice
A black storm broke, a howling tornado, its waterspout
Twisting and writhing, a monstrous phallus
Sucked down by the uterine sea. Driven off course,
Lay in doldrums with a broken rudder
Till rescue reached them—ignominiously towed
Into New York harbor by a scrawny little tug,
Triumphantly tooting.

                    Officially, of course,
He was slated to make the return passage home,
But early on caught emigrant fever and now
Jumped ship, went over the rail
Down a rope ladder to a fruit vendor's lighter

Tied alongside, hoping to hide under heaped produce.
Intercepted there, he dodged, sprang overboard,
And forthwith swam ashore.

                      And so, by the grace of God,
Entered America, an illegal alien,
Almost as if he too heard the call—
Fare Forward! Fare far!—almost as if
He too laid claim to a fabulous future
Uniquely his own.

                    The third of July, 1883.
Spending the first night under the docks,
He who had never heard tell of a firecracker
Woke next morning to the thunder of the Fourth.
Terrified, speaking no English,
Stumbling about the turbulent streets,
With no money and only the clothes on his back
For keeps, he persisted and survived.

                        Survived?
It was the first decisive act of his life,
And the most crucial. Heretofore, he had been
Only life's pawn, passively witnessing, moving but as
        moved.
Now, with one importunate stroke he cut free,
Severed the ethnic umbilical cord
To Norway and the past.

               After the first bewilderment
He caught the rhythm of the pulsing streets,
Found the company of his own kind,
The wild waifs who haunted the alleys,
Selling newspapers or shining shoes,
Pilfering, ganging up for mutual protection,
Perfecting a kind of pig-latin argot to faze the police,
Arcane confabulation in the cunning of the ruse.

*

From this point on his odyssey darkens.
He spoke of wanderlust, riding the freights
To other cities, rarer climes,
In the drifter's gambit. He once surmised
By the age of sixteen he had seen it all:
North, South, East, West: every section of the country
Duly transected, briskly shown the back of his heels,
The trace of his tracks, and him unscathed;
But that's to be doubted.

                    For it wasn't that easy.
In the first place, the competition was killing.
From the Civil War to the turn of the century,
Hardly thirty-six years, forty million people
Poured into America. They matted like herring
In the East Coast cities, invaded the Northeast,

Tied alongside, hoping to hide under heaped produce.
Intercepted there, he dodged, sprang overboard,
And forthwith swam ashore.

                        And so, by the grace of God,
Entered America, an illegal alien,
Almost as if he too heard the call—
Fare Forward! Fare far!—almost as if
He too laid claim to a fabulous future
Uniquely his own.

                    The third of July, 1883.
Spending the first night under the docks,
He who had never heard tell of a firecracker
Woke next morning to the thunder of the Fourth.
Terrified, speaking no English,
Stumbling about the turbulent streets,
With no money and only the clothes on his back
For keeps, he persisted and survived.

                            Survived?
It was the first decisive act of his life,
And the most crucial. Heretofore, he had been
Only life's pawn, passively witnessing, moving but as
        moved.
Now, with one importunate stroke he cut free,
Severed the ethnic umbilical cord
To Norway and the past.

                      After the first bewilderment
He caught the rhythm of the pulsing streets,
Found the company of his own kind,
The wild waifs who haunted the alleys,
Selling newspapers or shining shoes,
Pilfering, ganging up for mutual protection,
Perfecting a kind of pig-latin argot to faze the police,
Arcane confabulation in the cunning of the ruse.

                      *

From this point on his odyssey darkens.
He spoke of wanderlust, riding the freights
To other cities, rarer climes,
In the drifter's gambit. He once surmised
By the age of sixteen he had seen it all:
North, South, East, West: every section of the country
Duly transected, briskly shown the back of his heels,
The trace of his tracks, and him unscathed;
But that's to be doubted.

                      For it wasn't that easy.
In the first place, the competition was killing.
From the Civil War to the turn of the century,
Hardly thirty-six years, forty million people
Poured into America. They matted like herring
In the East Coast cities, invaded the Northeast,

Overflowed the Midwest, to span the Mississippi
And streak for California.

                    In the second place,
"Riding the rods" was a dangerous game,
In an age still largely harnessed to the horse,
Not fully acclimated to the stunning intrusion
Of locomotive speed: the intolerable wheels,
Iron on iron in the demon's dance,
Obsessively pounding a stupor in the brain;
The implacable distances, beckoning, fleering,
Disappearing over the fleeing horizon,
Stretching the nerves to the screaming point
In the rack of the body; malnutrition,
Common denominator of the hobo lifestyle,
Wasting the frame; death by maiming
Or prolonged exposure a foregone conclusion,
Everyone knew it but none could know when,
In a social structure the bottom of the heap,
The pit, the noxious human dregs: degenerate tramps,
Vicious police, and the loathsome
Ubiquitous jails.

                    Or so I believed.
And the litany of privations
Became my bane, a roster of risks
My sheltered beginnings could never match.
Rather, constrained by timidity,

Painfully introspective and unable to cope,
I winced in chagrin, bound by a febrile
Diffidence, awkwardly evasive. The misfit's onus
Shaped the poet's throttled cry.

                              But have lately learned
(Though indubitably he paid his freight-hopping dues
On the Atlantic seaboard and the nearer Midwest)
His coast-to-coast junkets were something else;
Those awesome forays were accomplished in style.
As companion to the secretary of James J. Hill,
Founder of the mighty Great Northern Line,
He rode the millionaire's private car,
Vicariously rich, hobnobbing with swells,
For all his abstention the surrogate sybarite,
Living high on the hog.

                              And the disparity
Staggers me. From the pits of privation
To the couches of ease; from the hazards of the body
To the surfeit of the soul, the revolution is complete.
For fortune itself is parlous; one can survive its lack
But hardly its largesse: brazen ostentation,
The masks of pride, envelope the unwary;
Complacence and superficiality,
Its pretentious habiliments, cannot conceal
The stark anatomy of greed: the gut of gluttony
And the groin of lust; the salacious copulation

Of money breeding money. In his randy youth
Surely he sensed the sexuality of power
And was stirred—knowing, drifter-wise,
How to hedge his hand, make his pitch, his ploy.
Intercourse with heiresses was not that unthinkable:
In their cloistered world proximity itself
Was potent, and here he was proximate.
All one needed was entrance, right?
And once in hand, once cunningly caught,
The bird could be plucked . . .

                    O my father!
What angel of deliverance watched over your ways,
Protected your head, guarded your heart
And guided your feet? What power kept you pure
Through the dizzying concentricities of that life?
Nameless the nights, incalculable the days,
The fierce temptations, inordinate succumbings,
And the gall of their wrenching guilts.

Or was it rather the primal austerity
Of the American earth that wrought privation
Into your soul? For you, a city child,
Lacked the sustaining context of Nature
That nurtured me. And listening at night
I heard, confirmed in the wind,
Roaming the vast shelvage of the Pacific Slope,
What I sensed in you: the innominate loneliness,

The sacred solitude that sustains the world,
The austere power that purified your lips
(I never heard you curse); that kept you sober
(I never saw you drunk); that made you honest
(I never heard you lie); the fierce abstractness
Denoting a primal equity, the chime of an absolute
Intrinsic to man.

           And women?
Which one seduced you, luring you out of that pall
Of birth-doom, to warm your blood
And shudder your heart? You were a faithful husband,
Scrupulously continent; but when I turned eighteen
You solemnly told me—the only sex instruction
You ever vouchsafed—"Go to a professional!"
Meaning, of course, a prostitute. It troubled me then
And puzzles me now. Whore-fucking
Is the last thing I can picture you doing;
But there it is, the sage advice
Of a lifetime's reflection! Which only shows
How little we know of our real life-sources;
How late we learn the reach of our roots,
Or the deeps of our blood's undoing.

But perhaps the thing is best understood
In the Victorian woman's view of herself
As invincibly chaste, inciting a corresponding
Violence in the legendary defloration,

Recalling Queen Victoria's rueful advice
To the British bride on her nuptial night:
"Close your eyes, my dear, and think of England!"
It threw the prostitute's amiable carnality
Into vivid relief, earning the visceral gratitude
Of numberless disenchanted males, her venereal sycophants.
From this point of view my father's
Hortatory admonition, far from denoting
A personal aberration, proved Rite of Passage
To a troubled generation.

*

                         He settled in time
In St. Paul, Minnesota, a Scandinavian enclave,
Where he found his trade: graduating as he grew
From street to shop, from newsboy to printer's devil;
Taken on as an apprentice compositor, novitiate
To the trade. Here he got his first education:
Typesetting, proofreading; learned the language in depth,
Plus the wide world of facts, to arrive
At journeyman's status, able to enter the skilled employ
Of any metropolitan daily in the country, a certified
Man of the stone.

                 But more to the point
Here too he found his calling. The distinction
Is vital. Just as his father

Sustained himself at the vulcanizer's bench,
But his calling was evangelical, so did the son
Sustain himself at the composing stone
Though his calling was music.

      Vocare! To be called
Is the definitive gist of vocation, and its implications,
For sensual artist or ascetic monk,
Are largely the same: each broaches
The charismatic mode. For intuition and instinct,
The Spirit and the Flesh, merge together
In worship and in art, shaping the radical
Contour of the visionary quest,
Ineluctably governed, not by the mind's
Inveterate lust for logic, but by the powerful
Suasion of symbolic truth, the force of vocation
Fusing the substances of soul and psyche
To the archetype of God.

      Call and surrender,
The dual foci of charismatic renewal.
Call is the first awakening of the self
To the stroke of potentiality. Surrender,
The abnegation of ego before the imperative
Of creative destiny, the clench of consummation.
No call, no surrender; no surrender,
No renewal. It is that simple.
And it can't be faked.

You have to wait for the call,
Wait out the terror of your helplessness
Before the deliverance of surrender.
Sometimes this takes years.
Sometimes, if you're lucky,
It takes decades.

*

How the call came to him
He never disclosed. A no-nonsense agnostic
Doubtless he never thought in such terms.
More than likely, hearing a band on a city street,
His being blazed, suddenly transfixed, an astounding
Awakening: the seizure of vocation
Coequals nature in elemental awe. I once saw a brace
Of Muscovy ducks, hatchery-raised far from a pond,
And fully grown before taken to water.
Shown the broad pool they crouched in distrust,
Must be shoved to the shore,
Nudged over the edge. But once afloat,
Overwhelmed by instinct, they gave voice.
What a long-deferred summons and what a surrender!
Such mad cavorting! Such diving and jubilant
Thrashing of wings! This, for my father, was music.
And music became his all.

                    In our beginning
Is our end. What he started then
He never forsook, never denied,
Never renounced. A true skald,
He was born to sing. In song
He lived, and singing
Died. Now I, his son,
Sing for him.

Canto Three
HIDDEN LIFE

DECEMBER 25, 1885, ADRIAN, MINNESOTA

And the hidden life: a farm girl born on Christmas Day
Out on the frozen Minnesota prairie,
Near the small town of Adrian,
In a Roman Catholic enclave,
Founded by the visionary prelate,
John Ireland, Bishop of St. Paul,
Who, in his greatness of heart,
Sought to draw the immigrant Irish
Out of the congested seaboard cities,
Where, given the appalling squalor of their lives,
Faith and morals stood in fearful jeopardy.
Urging them back to the land
He hoped to restore their Old World stability,
Here on the fertile American earth, the New Eden,
Under the boundless providence of God, and the vigilant
Eye of the Church.

                    An unmitigated disaster.
One stupefying Minnesota winter
Was enough to convince the feckless Irish

That their visionary prelate, though doubtless a saint,
Was balmy as a crumpet. Abandoning their homesteads,
They sold the implements he had generously provided,
Pocketed the money, and beat a ragged retreat
Back to the slothful seaboard cities,
Letting faith and morals take their chances
Where a body could keep warm.
This left the field to the Germans,
A more resolute breed.

                     And both strains
Blended in her blood: the father, a German,
For tenacity and earthiness; the Irish mother,
For piety and imagination. The mixture
Proved benign: the fourth child of ten
She spoke of her earliest years as the gladdest.
Though life was hard and poverty crippling,
The rewards of righteous family life
Proved recompense enough for the bone-bruising hardships.
Not forgetting the awesome presence
Of primary Nature, the stupendous
Magnitude of the earth, the vast sky
Gripped at the edge by the steel horizon,
Rim of the world.

                     *

     For there was always the wind,
Streaming, blowing across the limitless prairies,
Rattling the corn and the sunflowers,
Crying at night round the eaves of the house,
Calling the ghosts of the buffalo,
Stirring the dust of the pioneers,
And the shattered, sanguinary tribes.

       In the Spring
She remembered the wonderment over her brow,
Over her heart and her hovering breath,
Touching her body in unfamiliar places,
Of which she knew nothing, had been told nothing,
Strange yearnings for otherness,
The undulant urge of the fated unborn.

For there was always the wind.
It came up from the Gulf, out of Mexico,
From the Texas stretch and the Oklahoma hollow,
Brooding womb of tornados, those savage
Wreckers of railroads and cities,
Scarring the groin of Arkansas,
Coiling where rivers spawn and divide,
And birds of the night,
Tracing the shining tributaries,
Fly dazzled into the dawn.

     *

                    Then tragedy struck.
In her ninth autumn the death of her mother
Tore the family fabric and the cold rushed in.
The father was forced to send them away,
Divide his soul-stricken darlings,
Parcel them out among strangers.

Some he placed in a St. Paul convent,
My mother among them, but that winter they sickened
In the strange city, and had to be withdrawn.
Undaunted, he searched and found a convent
Closer to home, but fate still fought him.
They'd no sooner arrived when it burnt to the ground.
The distraught father had no recourse
But to place his children in such separate homes
As were willing to have them,
No questions asked.

                    Her own drab lot
Fell to a single-child couple in Adrian,
Where, separated from her sisters,
Her life turned miserable. She lay by night
Listening to the wind prowl round the house,
Menacing now, to rub its muzzle on the window pane,
Its voice a troll.

                    Baptized a Catholic
Her natal creed proved anathematic

To that insular household.
She stopped attending Mass to keep the peace
And, in effect, was raised a Protestant.
But rejoining her sisters one Summer vacation,
She received Confirmation and,
To the great indignation of her foster parents,
Returned to the Sacraments.
Soon active in her parish, helping the nuns
About the altar or in the catechizing of children,
She bore at home the irksome brunt of it,
And never wavered.

                    For prayer sustained her.
In the throes of that blunt familial estrangement
She found consolation in the sacramental life:
Slipping into church on her way about town;
Making the dolorous Stations of the Cross
Saturdays after Confession;
Receiving Holy Communion in her Sunday best
At the weekly Mass; praying the Rosary
Each night at bedtime, her fingers
Sifting the beads like nuggets of gold
In the wilderness of God; the words
Lilting her lips, moulding the mind
Till sleep tied her tongue
As the divine mantra closed. Let the troll wind
Whine at the windowsill; in the warmth

Of her inner world she found her solace,
And could not be shaken.

                    At fourteen years
She'd been taken from school and set to work
In the local newspaper — prefiguring my father there,
The man she would marry — setting type
And reading proof, folding the printed sheets
For delivery. This, too, her surrogate education,
Broadening her farm girl's limited outlook
With some knowledge of the world.
Bright, resourceful, she rapidly matured,
And knew satisfaction, confirming her worth
In the labor force, coming of age in the new century
That would bring the man to her.

                            He arrived,
As it happened, in the Wintertime, unannounced,
A Norwegian by birth but with no trace of an accent,
Goodlooking enough but not strikingly handsome
And short for his race. It soon developed
He was something special: the new bandmaster,
Belatedly hired by the town fathers
To present the next Summer's concerts,
Always, before the advent of radio,
The focal point of community interest
Through the long Summer months.

He had seen their ad in a city newspaper
And arrived for an interview. His credentials
Were impressive: he bore letters
From some of the best bands in the Midwest.
The salary was, let us say, adequate,
Provided they could secure him a place
On the local newspaper. It so happened they could:
The publisher, one of the pillars of the council,
Was pleased to oblige.

                    He took the acceptance
For granted; it had become by then
A way of life: he had learned it thoroughly,
Knew it inside and out, and himself as well,
Taking care to contract for one season only,
Since no small town had ever claimed him long,
But diplomatically agreed to renegotiate in the Fall,
If they liked him well and could come up with more money.

He would begin at once, whipping the callow band into
        shape
With weekly rehearsals toward the long Summer program.
That same day, in the newspaper printing plant,
He slipped on his denim compositor's apron
And stepped up to the stone.

                    *

                    And so they met,
Each finding the other consummately attractive.
For her, he brought fresh air, liberating life,
To that small town confinement.
He was well-read and knowledgeable,
With a fascinating past and intriguing future.
Clean of speech and of thought,
He was supportive and helpful,
Occasionally unloading her composing stick,
Though she was perfectly capable of that herself.
Moreover, she enjoyed correcting proof with him,
Herself reading copy while he skillfully marked
The ink-pungent galleys of freshly-pulled print.

For him, he recognized almost at once
She was everything he consciously valued in women:
A voice soft and low; cool, light laughter;
The gift of a keen sense of humor (a virtue
In which he himself was somewhat deficient)
But practical, too, adaptive and amenable,
Without affectation or self-preening vanity,
And implicitly honest.

                    In the Spring he proposed.
Nor was she surprised; for though she lacked amatory
Knowledge of men; indeed, had only
Superficially dated, on church outings,
Funfests, and suchlike sociables, her intuition

Read the signs and read them aright,
Recognizing the butterfly winging in his breast
By the chrysalis stirring in her own.

But there were grave problems.
She was Catholic and devout,
He, a confirmed agnostic.
She was fifteen years younger than he
And two inches taller. To make matters worse—
Indeed, to make them impossible—
He acknowledged in his past a failed marriage,
An ugly divorce.

          Oh, he could explain it!
Once, playing in a circus band,
He had fallen head over heels
For a female performer, a trapeze artist
And bareback rider, and they dashed into marriage.
He stressed the difficulties of circus life:
Incessant hoopla, the gypsy vagrancy,
Depthless euphoria and non-existent privacy.
And always crisis, crisis, the onslaught
Of the unexpected, from stampeding elephants
To irate farmers bilked of their money
By sideshow sharpers, the cry "Hey rube!"
Sending stake-swinging roustabouts
Charging out front to clip the yokels
Before they could rally and wreck the tents.

Add to this the hornblower's gantlet:
Playing cornet on lurching bandwagons,
Chipped teeth, lacerated lips and blood
Dripping out of the spit-valve. All this
They endured; but when times worsened
And circusing declined, she wouldn't settle,
Refused to bear children, twice aborting his progeny,
Till contention soured them beyond endurance,
And they parted in disgust.

                         (Grounds for annulment,
Under canon law, but difficult to prove,
And the diocesan chancery, given the options,
Declined to pursue it.)

                         Now he was alone,
Getting on in years, longing for a home
And the solace of a family. She, too,
Craved the love of a man and the wonder of a child,
And her heart was brimming, brimming.
But the thing was impossible;
The man didn't even believe in God.
To her credit she refused to lead him on.
She gave him no hope.

                         Then came the Summer.
Every Saturday night he stood on that bandstand
In his smashing white uniform,

Before the whole town and half the county,
And held them spellbound. He had fantastic presence,
And magical authority over a band.
He was, moreover, a sensational singer,
Specializing in the art of the Swiss yodel,
A popular showpiece performance of the day.
In short, he set the town on its ear.

Nor was she indifferent to that glamour;
Nothing in life had prepared her for it.
He haunted her sleep, and his daily presence,
Dominating the composing room, was almost maddening.
Yet despite her obsession she could not yield,
Was even, sometimes, secretly relieved
He was forbidden her: he was that compelling.

As for him, when the music stopped at Summer's end
And she remained adamant, he served notice and left.
He would not put in another such Winter.
If religion was her choice, the devil take her!
He knew what to do: find another city, another gig,
And yes, if he must, another woman.

                                          And the wind,
Blowing, took him away, gone across the prairie
In leaf-drift time, frost tracing the stubble,
Geese going south with the whooping cranes
In the smoky light of October.

Canto Four
THE HOLLOW YEARS

AUTUMNAL EQUINOX, 1905, ADRIAN, MINNESOTA

And so he was gone. And his absence
Imploded on that town like silence swallowing thunder.
She moved numbly through the shortening days;
Not an hour passed at the printing office
But his absence accosted her. She looked at the men
Seeing them stripped of their value,
Utterly ordinary, tedious in their humdrum insufficiency.
Where had the light gone? The Light
And the life?

      At the Mass,
Recalling his kisses, her prayers
Were cotton in her mouth. The keen-eyed nuns,
Who had not failed to note the tell-tale signs of one
Who could not say yes with her lips
But would not say no with her eyes,
Shook their heads and privately opined
That having dared to dance with the incubus

And tasted his lips, she must pay
Demon's debt with her pain,

                        And the pain came.
At Halloween a letter from a distant city
Limped in, for all the world like a bedraggled valentine,
All dejected spirit and wounded pride,
The rude awakening of the rejected swain.

He acknowledged himself miserable.
Never before had a woman so compellingly unstrung him.
He was sorry he had been so beastly precipitate.
If he could get back his job — that amenable
Bandmaster-compositor arrangement in Adrian,
Could he still be her friend? And if not,
(And here the mask slipped) since she obviously preferred
A life of prayer to living in love
Could she find it in her heart, say,
To pray for him?

                        It was a low blow.
Stung to the quick she shot back in anger:
Sorry that he suffered, but could he not understand
She was suffering too? Certainly she would pray for him,
Had been praying for him; but if God in His wisdom
Were to claim his wife, freeing him
(What dark expedients cross the mind when the heart is
        torn!),

Would he have gumption enough to pray for himself?
Let God be her judge if her bitter thoughts
Brought pain to anyone!

Thus two Victorians
Trammeled in the karma of the Great Divide
That separates the sexes.

In confession she learned that this correspondence
Was sinful. For her, the man must be outside the pale.
The least compromise was dangerous.
Put him out of your mind, girl. You are flirting
With the loss of your immortal soul.
The stakes are that crucial.

                              She wrote in distress,
One final time, begging him not to reply.
Still, he responded. Ignoring her admonition
He wrote bursting with news: the renowned
Saint Olaf's Band of Newbridge College,
Was slated to tour Norway, celebrating
The coronation of the new king, Haakon VII,
And the country's final independence
From the sovereignty of Sweden.
Louis had been approached to go, presumably
As a sort of ad hoc resource person,
His years as a barnstorming bandmaster
Marking him a natural for backup director,

Pinch-hitter and trouble-shooter par excellence,
Not to mention on-deck vocalist when occasion permitted.
Such virtuosity could prove a Godsend
For a musical organization travelling abroad.
This would be his first return to native turf,
And he thanked God for the chance, the rare opportunity
To prove himself to his people. How he wished
She could stand by his side
When he yodelled in the fiords of Norway!

                              Francelia
Was not amused. The irony of his thanking God
Had not gone unnoticed. How could she rejoice?
She had no such prospects: only the emptiness,
Only the grate of her dry thoughts
Abuzz in her brain; the past
A mocking memory; the future
A coffin and a corpse.

                    *

               She did not reply,
Determined to get on with her life.
Before she would hear from him again
Years would go by, her life would change,
Trouble would come to her, unhappiness deepen.
But she carried his memory and its meaning

Intrinsic to his being, wakeful within her,
His presence kept alive by what could only have been
Essentially her own: the substance of her faith.

*

For in the mating ritual of humankind
Priority of option resides with the woman:
The man can only ask. Why this should be so
Is a mystery of Nature. But reflection suggests
The mechanism of reproduction governs the game:
The fundamental uterine placement
At the base of sentient being. It is her consciousness
As the eyes and ears of the womb
That sets the sovereignty of selection
In the woman's hands. Of the working out
Reason may concur or sharply demur: it makes little
        difference.
Before it can even weigh its options,
Instinct has chosen, based on a swift
Connatural recognition, the subtle
Impact of an affinity like bonding,
Or the biological mystery of imprinting.
It is as father of her child
She chooses her mate. So here.
Before the ideological imperative preempting volition
Francelia chose Louis that I might be.

*

Do I go too far? Overstep the protective zone of humility
That garbs the psyche, preserves the soul?
But the quick of my life is the myth of my engendering.
Something was meant, something awesome and
          foreboding.
It tells me the gods are alive, they watch and are listening.
To live one's myth is to think in its terms.
To fulfill one's myth is to suffer through to its source.

*

That winter she sickened. It seems
One of her lungs had festered, the left one,
And she coughed up phlegm. No one could say
Just why, but later in her life she attributed it
To a casual incident in her middle teens.
At play with companions, she was frolicking
Around a kitchen table, girls with boys,
Playing tag, pushing and shoving,
When a lusty lad, reaching across the table,
Grabbed her arm and jerked her toward him.
She felt a tearing under her rib,
And in great pain she left the game,
But the hurt never healed though the pain ceased.
As time went by the matter worsened
And the doctors feared tuberculosis.
In any case, they advised, get out of Minnesota,
With its terrible winters. Go to California;

See what a change of climate can do.
This counsel daunted her, but in time she acquiesced,
Writing ahead to kinfolk in Los Angeles,
Alerting them she would be on her way.
When the time came she boarded that train
With a heavy heart, and left Minnesota forever.

*

Of the journey itself we know nothing.
She arrived in Los Angeles, presumably without incident,
Found lodging with her kin, and looked for work.
Presently she attended a beauty college,
Learning to be a manicurist, but forever afterwards
Kept mum about it. I couldn't imagine why.
But have lately learned that in those days the position
Was an adjunct of the barbershop, a masculine preserve,
Necessarily involving a certain presupposed
Intimate contact with casual men,
And though innocent in itself, it attracted
The demimonde who, like the parlor masseuse
Of our own day, exploited that intimacy
To turn a trick.

                Whether small town naïveté
Led her into it, she never said, but given her morals
That is the likeliest explanation. But it's just possible
That the contagious surge of big city freedom

Awakened her wild side, and, bridling
At the reins of respectability
She took her fling at living dangerously—
As a manicurist! Or perhaps her move
Was simple expedience: a way to meet men.
In any case she never acknowledged it. Her sisters
Spoke of her secretiveness (actually a close-mouthed
Capricornian attribute) and this is an instance of it,
Which she never quite lived down.

                                        Be that as it may,
It seems that her eyes began giving her trouble,
And she took to wearing glasses.
Later on, at a rooming house, the resident manager
Proved a Christian Scientist, one of the adept
Practitioners certified by the church. This woman
Persuaded her to set the troublesome glasses aside.
After an interval of prayer and meditation
Her eye problem cleared. Given a girl with a bad lung
This event proved eye-opening indeed. What is more,
Given a girl hopelessly in love with a man forbidden her,
Eye-opening intuition overnight became tunnel vision.

For the lady had faith. She herself had been healed,
And her countenance confirmed it: a spiritual aura
Pervaded her presence. For the girl Francelia
Faith was the indispensable requisite, the substance
She lived by. Then, too, other church members

Frequented the house, offering testimonials
Equally engrossing and no less credible.
For the church was strong in California. In fact,
    nation-wide,
It was at tide-crest, seizing the energies of the new century,
Its sensational novelty ripe for the times;
The electrifying news of its cures and conversions
Astounding the nation. In a very few days
Francelia attended her first service —
An act forbidden by her own church. And then began
Her first reading of *Science and Health* (also proscribed)
The controversial text of Mary Baker Eddy,
Charismatic founder and spiritual guide
Of the vital new movement.

                        Francelia was fascinated.
Familiar enough with the genre — Christian piety
And spiritual exhortation — she was unprepared
For what she found there: a singular earnestness
And down-home directness that were quite winning.
Reading on, she recognized clearly the faith-source
Of her landlady benefactress: the work rang true.
Couched in trite ecclesiastical diction, it concealed
An energy of startling originality:

> Prayer is not to be used as a confessional to cancel sin. Such an error would impede true religion. Sin is forgiven only as it is destroyed by Christ — Truth and Life. If prayer nurtures the belief that sin is cancelled, and that man is made better

> merely by praying, prayer is an evil. He grows worse who
> continues in sin because he fancies himself forgiven.

At first she had been non-plussed by the title.
Was it disingenuously misleading? The unwary reader
Handed a putatively medical text
Only to be regaled with religion?

As for the book's more problematical issue:
The Catholic charge of a radical
Quasi-Manichean denial of matter and the flesh
Contradicted by the Incarnation, she was too
      unsophisticated,
Too intellectually and critically undeveloped,
To take its measure.

      Rather, the more she read
The more she realized that here was a remarkable
Religious intelligence, a profound attempt
To restore the cutting edge of Christianity
To its original uses, powerful in its attributes
And decisive in its effects: a consummate achievement.
She was immensely impressed.

      But her commitment lay
  elsewhere,
And she knew it. Still, in all fairness, she owed it to herself
To objectively appraise the new challenge.

Buckling up her resolve she confronted the alternatives.
It did not take her long.

                      What the old church offered
She knew well enough, but its reward lay in the Afterlife.
What the new church offered was the same Afterlife,
The same God and the same Christ, but held out the promise
Of a healing here and now, on the strength, moreover, of a faith
She already possessed! The argument
Was irresistible. And her scrapped glasses,
Like hapless relics of defunct theologies,
Confirmed her deliverance.

                      True, her confessor,
Had she sought him out, would have forcefully admonished her,
Shaken by her patent transparency of motivation,
Pleading with her to reconsider. No upstart heretical sect
Could possibly replace the certitude
Possessed by the Church of Rome. No Mass. No sacraments.
No liturgy. No saints. And most telling of all,
No proven history of salvation. But when she remained
Obdurate in her resolve, withholding absolution
He would have sorrowfully given her his priestly blessing,
Wishing her well, and wondering what the Providence of God

Had in store for such an earnest soul, so young and so
    vibrant,
Yet given over to such abject self-deception.

*

What Providence had in store was a whole new scenario,
That was yet as old as the hills.
How Francelia and Louis found each other
We do not know, but find each other they did.
A photograph survives, taken "about the time
Of their marriage." It shows them in a park,
Presumably in California, on a Sunday afternoon —
One of those postcard pictures roving photographers
Took on holidays in public places,
Then sold you the print for fifty cents.
It was warm on that day. Louis, in shirt sleeves,
Has folded his coat across his arm,
And wears his straw hat back on his head
To cool his brow. His stance has the virility
Of a man sexually sure of himself, caught in a moment
Of unconscious definition. Francelia stands tall,
A little behind and above him, her superior height
Augmented by a slight rise in the ground.
She wears an old-fashioned seersucker dress,
White and cool-looking, and holds her hat before her
With both hands — not the token of repression,
Like the figleaf of Eve; but rather as a mandala,

Constellated at the zone of generation:
Passion's pit and the cleft of her fault.
Later, in her achieved maternity, other photographs
Will reveal her the classic madonna,
But now, on the eve of her nuptials,
The force of a subsumed freedom redolent in her figure,
She complements the man with a perky insouciance.
They are an impressive couple. I recall nothing
Quite like it among the family memorabilia.
It gives me an insight into something
Pondered a long time: one of the hardest things
The Oedipal son must come to understand
Is what the mother sees in the father.
For me, here it is, large as life:
What they found in each other. I own myself
Proud to be the spawn of this coupling.

*

They were married in Yuma, Arizona, on March 26, 1909,
Before a Justice of the Peace, and took up housekeeping
      there,
But not for long. Like an engendering flood the years
Swept them up and, circiling, left the eventual
Flotsam of their lives tracing their trek, the nightfalls
Of their sojourning. In 1910
Their first child, a girl, Vera Louise,
Was born in Phoenix, and the following year

Found them in Bakersfield, California, where I was
        conceived,
To be born William Oliver at Sacramento in 1912.
My brother, Lloyd Waldemar, saw the light of day
Only thirteen months later in Turlock.
When 1914 found them still farther south
In Fresno County, where the small town of Selma
Proved hospitable and warm, Francelia sensed
That this was the place and put down her foot.

Events proved her right: the famed
San Francisco-Panama Exposition of 1915
Saw the Selma Band in the main parade.
My father's hit tune, *Selma the Home of the Peach,*
Proved sensational, confirming at long last
His sense of identity with a specific locale,
And the wanderlust abated. He then relinquished
His newspaper job to found his own press,
The Everson Printery; but not until
They had purchased a lot and built a house
Did my mother feel we were home.

*

So came to a close the formative years
That set the stage for my entrance into life.
As I write, my feeling is one of awesome destiny,
But fearsome mischance as well:

One could so easily not have been born!
You tentatively feel of yourself,
Just to make sure you are really here,
That you do exist, the events of your life
Did actually happen, arriving at terminus
Ineluctably confirmed in the eschatological
Reckoning of who you are, to leave in your passing
As hidden increment, like quartz of the sea
On the glimmering strand, the pure distillate
Of the engendering flood.

Printed August 1990 in Santa Barbara & Ann Arbor for the Black Sparrow Press by Graham Mackintosh & Edwards Brothers Inc. Text set in Bembo by Words Worth. Design by Barbara Martin. This edition is published in paper wrappers; there are 300 hardcover trade copies; 150 hardcover copies have been numbered & signed by the author; & 50 numbered copies each with an original broadside poem printed by William Everson on handmade paper at the Kingfisher Press have been handbound in boards by Earle Gray & are signed by the poet.

Photo: Daniel O. Stolpe

WILLIAM EVERSON was born in Sacramento, California in 1912 and grew up in Selma, Fresno County, where he discovered his calling as a poet, married, and planted a vineyard. This idyll was broken by World War II, which he spent in Oregon work camps as a conscientious objector. His marriage did not survive the war, and thereafter he drifted to the Bay Area where he remarried and became involved in the celebrated San Francisco Renaissance but soon converted to Catholicism, necessitating a separation from his second wife. In 1951 he entered the Dominican Order as a laybrother, taking the name of Brother Antoninus, under which he became well known.

He left the Dominicans after eighteen years to remarry, and in 1971 became Poet in Residence at the University of California, Santa Cruz, retiring in 1981. He has published over fifty volumes of poetry and scholarship and is a handpress printer of distinction. His honors include a Guggenheim Fellowship, a Pulitzer nomination, the Commonwealth Club Silver Medal, the Shelley Memorial Award, the MLA Conference on Christianity's Book of the Year Award, the Robinson Jeffers Tor House Award, a National Endowment for the Arts Grant, the National Poetry Association Lifetime Achievement Award, the Oregon Institute of Literary Arts Award, and the PEN Center USA West, Body of Work Award. He lives with his wife and stepson in a cabin at Kingfisher Flat in the Santa Cruz mountains near Davenport, California.